THE SERIAL BURGLAR

By: Osama Alibrahim

There are times the devil himself becomes an angel and vice versa; could it be that he has something too dear to lose?

CHAPTER ONE

Las Marriot was taken approaching aback when he discovered his shop and bar had been broken into on a Monday morning in April. He was a middle-aged man in his forties. They lived in the village of Keswick, which is located in north-east St. Catherine. "I can't believe this," he exclaimed to his wife, Vita, who was also perplexed. Vita was a chubby woman of the same age as Las. She had given birth to four children for him: two girls and two boys. Vita had gotten up around six o'clock in the morning to get the kids ready for school. She'd gone to the store to get some ingredients for breakfast. She had turned on the lights and discovered items strewn about the floor. She alerted Las and the kids right away. Juby, their yard boy, had been dispatched to summon the cops. Las could think of a few people who could have robbed his business. Bender and Latty were two names that came to mind.

"Ladies, I don't think sending the kids to school today is a good idea," Vita said. "I'm sure all of this has shaken them up.

In fact, Las believes that we could all be dead right now. The kids had returned to sleep. Las and Vita walked to the shop's front door. They could see where the top bars of the shop's two large front doors had been plied apart, allowing a small child to pass through. The heavy doors had been re-entered. Las wished he had used bolts instead of padlocks on the doors.

“That's how it went down.” “Someone widened the steel bars with a crowbar and then pushed a young boy through,” Vita explained. Several people had now arrived on the scene. Jack Distant, who lived on the other side of the river, approached them. He told them, "I heard about it Las, last week they went in on Mundle and cleaned him out." They were startled to see a police car approaching them on the road. Sergeant Whitely, Corporal Morris, and Constable Ellis emerged from it. Las reasoned that Dick Lamey, the local district constable, was probably the only one left at the station.

He was taken aback because the cops didn't usually start working so early.

Perhaps the recent spate of break-ins had prompted them to begin working earlier than usual. “Can you tell me what happened here, Las?” Sergeant Whitely was the one who in�uired. “Vita went into the shop to get some breakfast for the kids before they went to school when she discovered the break-in.”

The Sergeant pulled out his notebook and started writing. “There have been a number of break-ins recently. Mundle was robbed, and Miss Trina and Mister Deacon's shops were both broken into in the last week, according to Whitely. “We suspected Latty and went after him, but he was unarmed. We searched his home and even stationed Dalby to keep an eye on him, but to no avail,” Corporal Morris reported. Morris drew a sharp look from Whitely. He didn't understand why Morris was yelling that Dalby was one of their spies when he was well aware of the general contempt for informers and the dangers that the job entailed. “Come on, Las, let's go into the shop and bar.

I'll give you a heads up not to touch anything. As they entered the shop, Whitely told Las, "I've called Spanish Town, and they'll be sending a detective up here to do some fingerprinting."

The lights in the shop were turned on by Las. Things were strewn all over the floor, as could be seen. Las told the cops, "They took all my cigarettes and all the li�uor they could find." Corporal Morris stated, "You can bet that someone will buy those things from these robbers." “I'll have to get Dick Lamey to visit a few of the shops and bars in Keswick, Nelson, and Howell's Content,” says the author. Sergeant Whitely said, "I'm sure he'll pick up something." As they approached the bar, they could see that what Las had said was correct. Before returning to the Keswick police station, the three officers stopped to eat some of Vita's breakfast. Las was at a loss for what to do next. He installed stronger burglar bars and padlocks the next day. With his machete in his hands, he was now sleeping. Dalby had been hired to assist him, and Juby had been hired to keep an eye on the shop and bar.

“Las, let's go after them. We could apprehend one of those lads and ask him what they were up to out here.”

Both of them dove into the gully. They dashed down to the Keswick River, but the boys and Bender were already floating downstream. They dashed along the river's edge and dove into the water. Bender leaped from the water and dashed into the undergrowth. “Let's keep these lads in check, Dalby. We'll have another chance to catch Bender. Perhaps these lads can tell us what they were doing out here at this hour.” The two boys attempted to flee, but Las and Dalby were far too ⍰uick for them. They snatched both boys from the water and dragged them out. The boys were familiar to both Las and Dalby. Lippy was the name of the taller boy, and Fred was the name of the shorter boy. Both boys appeared to be around twelve years old, Las thought. “What are you guys doing out this early in the morning?” Las was adamant. Both boys were deafeningly ⍰uiet. Dalby went for a massive stick that was lying on the riverbank. He threatened, "Talk or I'll beat both of you with this stick."

“We'll take them to the police station,” says the driver. Maybe they'll be able to persuade them to speak.” Las noticed that neither of the boys seemed alarmed by his threat to take them to the police station. He noticed that neither of the boys' expressions had changed. “The cops are powerless to help us. Lippy protested, "We didn't steal anything from anyone." “What are you guys doing with us? We haven't made any mistakes. My father has gone in search of his weapon. He stated that he would go for it. He'll shoot both of you if he comes back and sees you holding us like this,” Fred warned. “He's bluffing you, Las,” says the narrator. “As far as I know, Bender doesn't have a gun,” Dalby countered.

“We're going to the police station with them.” “Let's take them down.” Las, on the other hand, was not having it. As a result, the boys were marched up the road. They decided to leave the boys at Las' house because it was still early. When Las and Dalby took the two boys up to the police station, they were in for a rude awakening.

They claimed they had been kidnapped by Las and Dalby. When Las and Dalby came down and held them, they had gone to the river for an early morning swim and to catch shrimps. They were accused of attempting to break into Las' shop and bar. They were going to do the burglary with Bender, he said. Las shook his head when Corporal Morris asked if he saw the boys commit the crime. They saw the boys and Bender running down the road, according to Dalby. The corporal informed them that he could not charge the boys with anything. Both boys threatened to stone Las and Dalby as they walked home through the station yard. Las chose to stay at the police station and converse with the officers. He revealed that the boys' true intention was to break into his shop and bar once more. Las believed the cops were more concerned with apprehending Bender. They had no desire to detain his sons. Dex, a local farmer, drove up just as he and Dalby were leaving the station yard and offered them a ride in his pickup. They'd driven about a □uarter of a kilometer when Las spotted Lippy and Fred on a hill, stacking massive rock stones.

Dalby had been spotted in the back of the pickup by the boys! They began to pelt him with stones. Dex slammed the brakes on the pickup and jumped out. "Hey, you guys, are you crazy or something?" He'd taken a machete from the back of the pickup truck. Las had also exited the vehicle.

"Throw any more stones down here, smash up my car, and see what I can do to you boys." "Dex, it's Las and Dalby we're after," Lippy yelled. "Drive away and leave them to us," Fred advised Dex, "so we can hit them with our stones." Las and Dalby each took a pickaxe and a digging bill from the back of the van. They raced up the hill after the two boys, together with Dex. Lippy and Fred had spotted them approaching and dashed down a gully into the bushes. They were pursued by Las and Dalby, who threw stones at them. Las doubted that any of the stones had struck either of the boys. When Las returned home, he informed Vita of the events at the police station. He kept her in the dark about the fight with Bender's sons.

Bender had been spotted two days later, but he had once again escaped into the bushes. Las considered going after Bender on his own, but he would re�uire assistance. He discussed it with both Vita and Dalby. Vita was cautious, while Dalby was enthusiastic. “I heard Bender has a long gun, Las,” says the narrator. He'll use it to shoot you. I heard Hep Johnson had misplaced his gun. I'm not sure if it's the gun Bender took. Las, please don't leave. I don't want him to be the one to kill you.” Las assured Veta that Bender didn't have a gun. True, he'd heard Hep's gun had been stolen, but he didn't believe it was Bender's fault. Las discussed his plans to track down and capture Bender over the next few days in private.

Several of his friends warned him that such a scheme would be dangerous. Bender was not a threat to Las, he assured them. He explained that he didn't want word of his attempt to capture Bender to reach Bender. As a result, Las began to prepare for the adventure. He decided to bring Dalby along. Dalby was a lightning-fast runner despite his diminutive stature.

Bender, as far as Las knew, was lightning fast. He once outran a police jeep before diving down a gully and disappearing into the thickets. With or without Bender, they planned to leave on Friday morning and return by Sunday evening. In primary school, Las was a scout, and in high school, he was a cadet. As a result, he had spent a lot of time camping. They'd bring sleeping bags, enough food to last three days, and cooking utensils. Las and Dalby each brought a machete and a well-cured piece of pimento stick with them. They also brought a rope with them in case they caught Bender. Vita's eldest sister and her two teenaged boys and a young girl arrived on Thursday evening to stay with them. They would assist her in the shop while Las was away. During the three days, Juby would keep an eye on the shop and bar.

CHAPTER TWO

So, on Friday, Las and Dalby set out for Lobban's Ridge's woods. Keswick was about five miles away from Lobban's Ridge. To get to the Woods, Las and Dalby had to walk the entire distance. They had walked a mile when they were suddenly pelted by huge stones. "What the hell, Bender's boys are attacking us!" yelled Las. "Las, let's get behind those trees!" Dalby, for his part, yelled as they dashed for a nearby grove of trees. The trees were being built, but the stones were getting closer. "What are we going to do now, Las?" "They'll keep us penned in here until tonight if we don't attack them," Las predicted. "Let's get some stones and throw them at those boys," says the group. As far as I can tell, there are two of them," Dalby said. As there were stones behind the grove of trees, they began to gather them. Before darting back to their hideout, Dalby and Las would throw stones at the boys. They had already thrown several stones when one of the boys began to cry. Before they heard running footsteps, another person began to cry.

Las and Dalby rushed out of hiding, determined to apprehend and beat the boys. They dashed to the boys' location, but all they found was a heap of stones. The boys were seen jumping down gullies. “Let's chase them down and beat them up for stoning us. “It's Lippy and Fred,” said Las. They were startled to see two larger boys running towards them. Both boys had clubs in their hands. As he and Dalby turned to face a new threat, Las thought to himself, "These boys look like grown men." Despite this, they were familiar with the boys' names. Boysie was the name of the older boy, and Delly was the name of the younger boy. “You dirty fuckers, you and Dalby threw stones at Lippy and Fred, knocking them down. Boysie screamed and attacked Las, saying, "We're going to beat you up for that." Delly used his stick to attack Dalby. The two boys who were holding their own against Las and Dalby were fighting them. They couldn't afford to let these boys beat them up, Las realized. Boysie and Delly would almost kill them if they defeated them. They were going to leave them for Bender to finish. Las became more aggressive in his fighting, and Dalby began to push the boys back. Boysie abruptly turned and bolted.

Delly jumped down a gully after his brother. As they raced through the thick bushes, they heard both boys breaking twigs. “We have to track them down, Las. For all the trouble they've caused us, they deserve a beating,” Dalby said. “Those lads are a nuisance. I'm wondering if Bender is employing them to divert our attention away from him. We've already lost about four hours. Let's get on with what we came here to do,” Las suggested. “I didn't realize Bender had so many kids. Dalby opined, "It's no surprise he has to steal so much to feed them." Las was perplexed as to why these women had so many children for Bender. He and Dalby went to get their belongings and resumed their journey. They made it to the Woods without incident. Those boys would have realized they couldn't compete with them. Las, like Dalby, had taken some hard blows in their most recent fight. Those lads had also taken some hard knocks. Both sets of boys had been injured, forcing them to flee, and Las knew it. They arrived at the Woods around 2:00 p.m. that afternoon. For several miles, the Woods ran. Several rivers and springs ran through the area.

There were fruit trees, some of which were in full bloom, such as mangoes and apples. Dalby picked some fruits from an apple and then a mango tree. Before continuing, he and Las sat in the shade and ate some of the fruits. They continued, deciding not to cut down any trees or bushes that might reveal their location. Las knew they needed to get to the Dawson River and wait for Bender there. They stopped by a river for roasted breadfruit, fried pork, and ackee for lunch. Dalby picked the ackees and breadfruits from their respective trees.

They set off again after eating and filling their canteens. Las wondered aloud if Bender had been notified as they moved through the bushes. They couldn't find any trace of the man. He wondered if they'd come back empty-handed. Las was also concerned about his loved ones. Let's say Bender slipped through the cracks and attacked them in the shop. They couldn't go back, he knew. Although he knew Vita's sister and her children would be no match for Bender and his boys, he was glad they were staying with them.

Juby was useful, but he, too, would not be able to stand up to them. That night, they slept in a grove of trees. Dalby was the first to put on his watch. They set out the next morning after breakfast. They'd been walking for about a mile when they came across a larger grove of trees and heard voices calling out to them. Dalby was told to keep quiet by Las. They crept closer to the clearing. Breakfast was being eaten by a group of men who were sitting on some large rocks. Clinch Salmon and his sons, Welly and Macky, were there! Fuller and Luddy were the other two men present. So this was the Salmon gang's base of operations, Las reasoned. Clinch was armed with a large axe and a long gun. Las had no idea what kind of weapon it was. Welly and Macky were wielding long machetes, and Las wasn't sure if they were armed. Steel clubs and short machetes were carried by both Fuller and Luddy. If Las and Dalby were discovered, they would almost certainly die. Clinch Salmon was in his early fifties, and his sons were in their early twenties, according to Las. Fuller and Luddy were in their mid-thirties when they met. Clinch was a ruthless robber with a reputation for being ruthless.

He'd robbed in all of the villages and even served time for it. His sons had spent their childhoods in reform schools. Fuller and Luddy were bare-faced criminals who had served multiple robbery sentences. “We're going to clean out Juville's and Toby's places tomorrow. Clinch told them, "That should net us about fifty thousand dollars." “Can you tell me when we're going to Noddy's?” Welly was the one who in⍰uired. “You've seen what Noddy has on his farm,” says the narrator. He has a lot of goats, pigs, and cows, as well as a lot of produce and tree crops, which he watches over like a hawk. On that farm, he has about three guns. With only one gun, we couldn't fight him.” “Are we going to leave that one alone?” Luddy in⍰uired. Clinch erupted in laughter. He took a big bite out of an ackee and saltfish sandwich, chewed it up, and then drank some coffee to wash it down. “I never said anything like that. You're all aware that I never give up on a project. Those farmers must either pay me protection money or I will raid them. In terms of Noddy, once we get some more guns, we'll attack and wipe him out.” Las and Dalby had to cover their noses even from where they were hiding. They had to hold their stomachs in fear of puking up their most recent meal. The five men were a stench. Their clothes were filthy and ragged. Their hair was tangled and filthy as well. With so many rivers nearby, Las couldn't imagine men walking around smelling like that. There was also a soap bush. Las hadn't brought any soaps with him and instead relied on the soap bush. Dalby, he knew, had done the same thing. The meal was finished in another ten minutes. Clinch and his gangsters revealed a lot of information during this time. Clinch had the gun that had been stolen from Hep Johnson, they revealed.

Clinch also gave them the names of all the gun owners in the village. He also stated that some of those guns should be in the hands of his gangsters. Las awaited his name to be called as a potential future victim. Clinch's silence on the subject provided him with no comfort. Perhaps Bender had returned some of the items he had taken from him. Las and Dalby crept away as soon as the meal was finished. When Las spoke, they were about a mile apart.

“I don't think we'll be able to get Bender out of these bushes,” says the narrator. I don't think we'll be able to get past Clinch and his gang.” “We have to give it our all. We can move Bender out at night once we get him,” Dalby said. They continued on their journey. They came across the remains of fire about a mile further. Las looked over the ashes. They were cold, and the fire was small in comparison to the one started by the Salmon gang. Bender had to have stopped for a meal, and it was either late last night or early this morning, Las had to assume. They noticed some tree limbs being cut down and deduced that the man was moving �uickly and may not be aware that he was being pursued. They ate late and decided to spend the night in a valley. They were so exhausted that they fell asleep almost instantly. It was bright sunshine when they awoke on Sunday morning.

Dalby went straight to work looking after breakfast. They packed their belongings and left after finishing their meal. They arrived at a clearing an hour later. There was a man on a hill off in the distance.

It had to be Bender! “Las, it's Bender!” exclaims the narrator. Dalby yelled. “If we want to catch him, we have to leave our gear,” Las advised. “They're going to take them.” However, Las stated that they had to conceal their belongings. Before going after Bender, they hid them in some bushes. They had only traveled a short distance when they realized he had seen them and began sprinting. Las and Dalby were the ones who came after him. They couldn't let Bender get to the Dawson River and his rope ladder, Las realized. Las and Dalby were both bad swimmers. They wouldn't be able to cross that river, Las knew. Bender was putting more distance between himself and his assailants. Las was sprinting away from Dalby, who was trailing behind. Dalby caught up with him �uickly. They were a few yards behind Bender when he flew around a tree; Dalby followed him but fell over an edge into a spring.

Las followed Bender around the tree, but he sped away. Las was well aware that he was the only one who could defeat Bender. They were a mile or so from the river.

Bender was now about a �uarter of a mile ahead of him. Las was unsure if he'd be able to catch him.

Bender was making progress, but he was exhausted, and Las was closing in on him. Dalby had emerged from the spring, but he was already too far behind. Las knew he couldn't let Bender get to the river's low banks, where he could throw himself into the water. Bender was now a few yards from the river's low banks. Las was well aware that he needed to act. He lunged at the man's legs, but Bender swerved away. Dalby dove at his legs just as he was about to throw himself into the river. The two men rolled to the bank's edge and then crossed. Las and Dalby had jumped over the riverbank and were holding Bender.

Bender fought the two men for a while, but they eventually got the upper hand on him. “You're not going to get away with it, Las. And you, Dalby, just wait until I'm free to see what I'll do to you. “I'm going to kill you both.” He then burst out laughing.

“You guys are a bunch of idiots. This forest is under the control of Clinch Salmon. He's a friend of mine. You're not going to get me past him and his gang. The best advice I can give you both is to get these ropes off of me and get out of here before Clinch and his gang find out you're here.” “Bender, we're bringing you in. Las told him, "We intend to get past Clinch and your boys."

He and Dalby led Bender to their respective packs. They piled their belongings into their backpacks and walked away, pushing their prisoner in front of them. Dalby's worried expression caught Las' attention. He was well aware that the man was apprehensive about meeting Clinch and his sons. Clinch would be informed of their presence in the Woods by Bender.

They ate their supper that evening and slept in a bamboo grove. Las and Dalby agreed to alternate watching. They ate breakfast before continuing their journey. When they came across some thick woods, Las and Dalby, along with the reluctant Bender, moved through the bushes.

Las walked over to the trees and peered through them. There was a structure there, Las thought, that looked like a shack.

Bender yelled, "You've found Clinch's house!" Las motioned for him to stop shouting, but the man refused. "Only Clinch, his boys, and I are familiar with this location. If he finds you here, he'll kill you." Las threw the rope tying Bender to Dalby and went inside the house to investigate.

The house's front door was unlocked. Las pushed the door open and entered. To get more light, he opened the board windows. Las noticed that there were four lofts with ladders leading up to them for sleeping. There was a table with some shabbily constructed chairs. Two bancras had their clothes hanging out of them. The room had a sparsely furnished interior. Las exited the building. He gave Dalby a signal. “It is, after all, a hideout. We have to get out of here as soon as possible if it's Clinch's.”

CHAPTER THREE

They gathered their belongings and set out, pushing the hesitant Bender ahead of them. He was shuffling his feet and yelling that he didn't want the ropes around his neck. Two men jumped down on them as they were leaving another grove of trees. Mackie, Fuller and Clinch's older son, was one of them. “What are you guys doing here?” says the narrator. Fuller was adamant. “What do you think we should do, Fuller?” Las, in turn, inquired.

“Las was just snooping around your hideaway. “He says he's going after the cops,” Bender explained. “What! How did he find the shack in the first place? Bender, you showed them?” Bender was fingered by Mackie with an accusatory finger. Fuller speculated, "Probably sold us out so they could take those ropes off him." “How could I have done it? Bender protested his innocence, saying, "They have me bound and say they're making a citizen's arrest."

“Let's keep these lads occupied until Clinch arrives. As he and Mackie attacked Las and Dalby with huge sticks, Fuller said, "He'll know what to do with them." Las and Dalby took up their sticks and engaged the two men in combat. Before Clinch and the rest of the gang returned, Las knew they had to beat up the two men.

“Can you tell me where Clinch is?” Las inquired as he pounced on Fuller and smacked him across the face with his hand. The man screamed in pain but did not drop his stick. As he attacked Dalby, Mackie yelled, "I'm going to beat you up!" Las and Fuller, as well as Dalby and Mackie, were fighting ferociously. Las had landed some hard blows on Fuller and thought he'd finished him off, but the man kept coming back. “I'm going to arrest you, Las. Keep you here until Clinch comes back to kill you.”

As he rushed the man, Las yelled, "You won't be that lucky, Fuller." Mackie suddenly yelled. “He's shattered my hand.” When the man groaningly collapsed to the ground, Las witnessed it. “Bender is attempting to flee, Las. “I'm pursuing him.” Las was too preoccupied with fighting Fuller to respond. Las was relieved because the fights with Bender's sons had given him a much-needed break. He knew that if he didn't beat Fuller soon, he'd have to fight Clinch. Las and Fuller were squabbling wildly. Las had delivered some lusty blows to the man and had received some in return. Las was closing in on the man and punching him in the face. As Fuller moved, Las dummied a blow and delivered a powerful blow to his left leg. The man screamed, "You've broken my foot!" and collapsed to the ground. Las came crashing down on him. Dalby was leading Bender back.

“You let Las and Dalby beat you up, Fuller and Mackie. Clinch will expel you both from his gang.” “Take a look at who's talking. “How did you allow them to bind you with a rope?” With a sneer, Mackie inquired. Dalby and Las got some wisp rope and tied Fuller and Mackie to different trees. They then gathered their belongings and resumed their journey, pushing Bender ahead of them. They came to a halt about two hours later for a rest and a meal. When they heard gunshots, they started moving again. It sounded like it was coming from the depths of the forest. Bender speculated, "That's Clinch, he's probably come back and found his boys beaten and tied up and is letting off steam." “Shut up, Bender,” Las said, threateningly waving his stick at him. “You're going to hell, Las,” says the narrator. Clinch will undoubtedly give both of you boys to me to beat.” Bender's taunts were ignored by both men. Las knew they had to keep going.

They could hear motor vehicles passing by an hour later, and they knew they would soon be on the road. Las decided to take another break and eat a snack.

“My boys are all over the place, ladies. They're not going to let you in without a fight.” “We've already fought two sets of your boys. We thrashed them with our sticks. Some of them threw stones at us, but we returned fire and knocked down two of them,” Dalby explained. As they gathered their belongings and re-started their journey, Bend threatened, "I'll get both of you for what you did to my boys." “With sticks and stones, your boys attacked us. What did you expect us to do, lie down and let them trample on us?” “He hasn't told us what he did with the goods he stole from you, Las, up until now. And why was he, Lippy, and Fred trying to break into your house the other day and shop?” Bender yelled, "You're just a police informer, Dalby!" “He won't be able to hide them in time.

When the cops raid his hideout this time, they're almost certainly going to find some of those items." "You're going to hell, Las. Because they won't find anything at the shack, the cops will let me go. I'm going to hire a good lawyer and file a lawsuit against you. He mocked, "I'd sue Dalby too if he didn't have any money." They'd made it to the main road. "I'm hoping we don't run into any of those lads again." As they set off up the road, Dalby declared, "I'm tired of fighting them." They still had a five-mile walk ahead of them. Las hoped they could get a taxi, but he knew they were hard to come by in these parts. He was also considering whether or not they should wait until nightfall to leave Bender. They risked being discovered by Clinch and his gang if they stayed in the bushes. The lesser of the two evils, Las reasoned, was facing Bender's boys.

Las and Dalby were on high alert for Bender's sons as they walked up the hill.

They came around a corner and saw some boys on a small playfield playing football. Four of the boys left the game after Bender yelled at them. None of these boys were familiar to Las or Dalby. “Get me away from these men, Josh and Bissy,” Bender yelled at the two older boys. The boys ran and grabbed sticks at Bender's re�uest. Las estimated that the boys' ages ranged from fifteen to nineteen. Las and Dalby were pitted against two boys each. Other boys stood nearby, but they had no relation to Bender. Bender re�uested that some of the onlooker boys cut the ropes, but they refused. The four boys were fighting Las and Dalby. Dalby was given some instructions by Las. Bender was yelling commands to his sons. One of the boys fighting Las dashed to get a large stone to throw at him. Las then slammed his fist into the other boy's leg. The youngster clutched his leg, cried out, and ran away.

Las deflected the huge stone thrown at him by the other boy, but then he heard Dalby scream. "They broke my hand, Las," says the narrator. When the two boys rushed down on Dalby, Las noticed. As the two boys pounced on Dalby, Bender yelled, "Beat up Dalby, kill him, Josh and Beppo!"

Suddenly, a pickup truck came around the corner and came to a complete stop. The driver and another man exited the vehicle. It was Dex, and the other man was Tanny, a local farmer. When Dex and Tanny ran to get machetes from the back of the pickup, the two boys who were beating Dalby bolted. When Dex pursued the boy who was stoning Las, he stood his ground but fled.

What had happened, Las explained. Despite Bender's protests, he and the injured Dalby were loaded into the pickup.

However, just as they were about to drive away, a group of men emerged from the bushes further down the road. Clinch, Luddy, and Welly Salmon, to be exact! "Drive, Dex!" exclaims the narrator. From the back of the pickup, Las yelled. They sped away after Dex started the pickup. Clinch fired his gun, and Las and Dalby ducked. Bender's head had to be held down by Las. Clinch fired another shot, but the bullet flew right through their heads. The shooting came to a halt as they rounded a corner. Las and Bender were dropped off at the police station by Dex. Corporal Morris, on the other hand, said he had summons for Las and Dalby there.

Apparently, the mothers of Fred and Lippy, as well as Boysie and Delly, had issued summonses against them for injuring their sons. The corporal informed them of their court date and urged them to appear.

When Bender's sons failed to appear in court two weeks later, Las and Dalby were released.

Bender was re-arrested, and he was charged with a slew of new offenses. He was sentenced to five years in prison. Las and Dalby were successful in leading the cops to Clinch Salmon's hiding place. His gang was eventually apprehended by the police, and each member was sentenced to various prison terms. Dalby received Las' share of the reward money for the capture of both Bender and Clinch Salmon. Dalby and his wife were able to open a shop in a nearby neighborhood with this money.

Some of Benders' ten sons followed in their father's footsteps, but others, seeing what had happened to him, chose a different path. His three daughters have all gone on to become professional women and live in different parts of the world.

Despite everything that has occurred, Las remains concerned about what will happen when the Salmon gang and Bender are released from prison. He has, in fact, purchased a gun and is putting it through its paces in preparation for that eventuality.

Made in the USA
Columbia, SC
01 August 2021